For Jack Griffiths and Robert McLaughlin
—A.D.

For Harvey
—R.C.

tiger tales

an imprint of ME Media, LLC

202 Old Ridgefield Road, Wilton, CT 06897

Published in the United States 2008

Originally published in Great Britain 2007

by Oxford University Press

a department of the University of Oxford

Text copyright © 2007 Alan Durant

Illustrations copyright © 2007 Ross Collins

CIP data is available

Printed in China

ISBN-13: 978-1-58925-412-1

ISBN-10: 1-58925-412-0

Billy Monster's DAYMARE

by Alan Durant   illustrated by Ross Collins

tiger tales

In a darkish, creepy wood…

in a darkish, spooky house...

in a darkish, gloomy bedroom...

there was a...

The bedroom door creaked open.

"What's wrong, Billy Monster?" Daddy Monster
growled softly. "Did you have a daymare?"

Billy Monster nodded.

"Yes," he said, sobbing. "I dreamt I saw a . . .

a child!"

"Oh dear," said Daddy Monster. "You poor baby."
"It was a boy child," said Billy Monster, "with two little eyes, and two little ears, and no horns at all!"

"Ugh," said Daddy Monster. "That IS horrible."

Daddy Monster tucked in
Billy Monster again and howled
a monster lullaby until Billy
Monster fell asleep.

Then Daddy Monster crept away, shutting the door behind him, and went back to bed.

He had just started to gurgle and snore when…

"Oh, Billy," growled Daddy Monster sleepily. "Not another daymare?"

"Yes," said Billy Monster.

"Was it a child again?" asked Daddy Monster.

"Yes," said Billy Monster. "It was a girl child. She had horrible yellow hair and a tail at the back of her head. And she tried to kiss me!"

"Oh no!" cried Daddy Monster. "That is REALLY awful. That is the worst daymare of all. You poor darling."

Daddy Monster gave Billy Monster a cup of cold slime.
Then he stroked his horns soothingly until Billy Monster
began to dribble and hiss.

Daddy Monster went back to
his own bed once more.
But no sooner had he started
to slobber and grunt when...

AIIIIIIEE!

"What is it now?" Daddy Monster groaned wearily.

"I think...I think...there's a child in my room," wailed Billy Monster. "Over there behind the curtain."

He pointed to the window where there was a tiny gleam of daylight.

"I'll check," said Daddy Monster, and he pulled back the curtain....

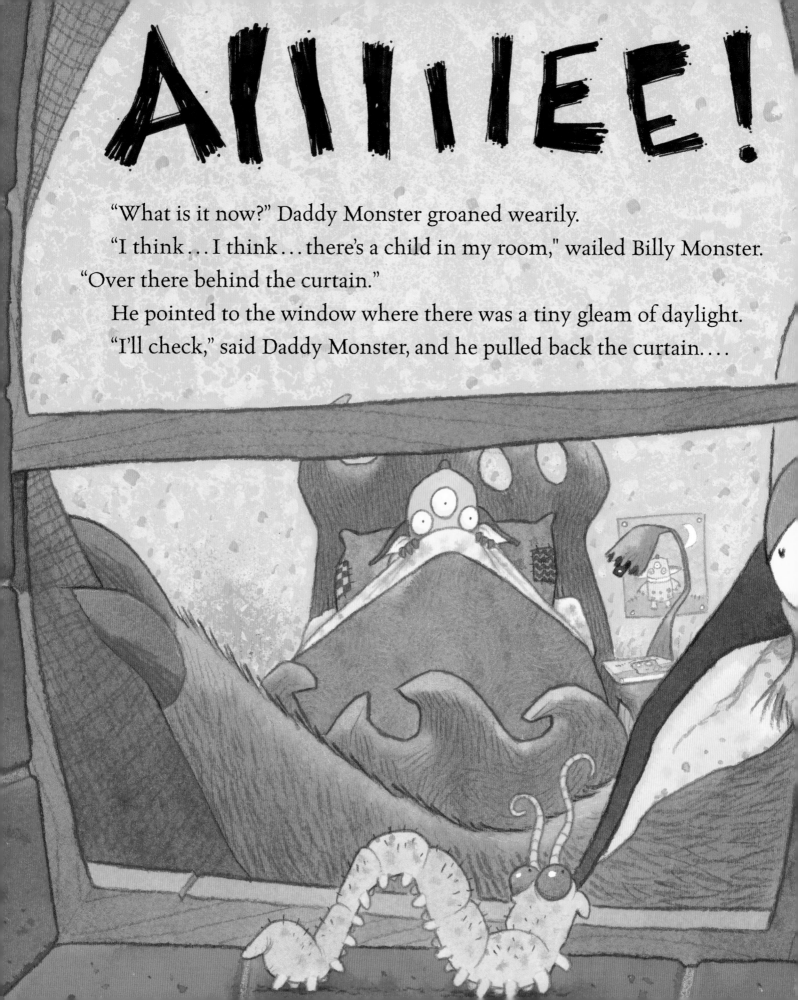

"There's no child here," he said. "See? It was just the branches of the tree you saw. It's too light in here, that's the problem."

Daddy Monster drew the curtain across so that the window was completely covered.

"That's better. Now it's nice and dark," said Daddy Monster.

"Thank you," Billy Monster said in a wobbly voice. "But…could you look in my closet, too, please?"

Daddy Monster looked in the closet...

and on top of the dresser...

and behind the bookcase...

and under the bed.

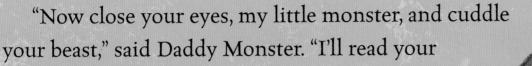

"Nope," said Daddy Monster. "No child in here. There's no child anywhere except in your head. Children aren't real."

"Oh," said Billy Monster. But he didn't sound very sure.

"Now close your eyes, my little monster, and cuddle your beast," said Daddy Monster. "I'll read your favorite bedtime story."

"*Once upon a time there was a brave little monster,*" Daddy Monster began.

He read about how one brave little monster met some children one night and wasn't scared at all. They made friends and played spooky games together. Then they all went back to the little monster's house and ate slug-and-eyeball stew.

"And the brave little monster lived happily ever after," said Daddy
Monster, closing the book. "Now go to sleep, *my* brave little monster."

Daddy Monster gave Billy Monster a big monster kiss....

SLUUUURRP!

He was just opening the bedroom door when Billy Monster asked very softly, "Well, just supposing there was such a thing as children... do you think they'd have bad dreams about monsters?"

Daddy Monster rolled
his eyes and laughed.
"Oh, Billy!" he said, with a snort.
"What a silly Billy you are! Why...

who

could

scared

of

ever

be

us?"